Inspired by
Danni and Mac.

May you always believe in your
total awesomeness.

www.mascotbooks.com

Finn Beloomey and His Great Big Giant Ears

©2018 Deena Sullivan. All Rights Reserved. No part of this publication may be reproduced, stored in a retrieval system or transmitted in any form by any means electronic, mechanical, or photocopying, recording or otherwise without the permission of the author.

For more information, please contact:
Mascot Books
620 Herndon Parkway #320
Herndon, VA 20170
info@mascotbooks.com

Library of Congress Control Number: 2018902720

CPSIA Code: PRT0718A
ISBN-13: 978-1-68401-061-5

Printed in the United States

FINN BELOOMEY
AND HIS
GREAT BIG GIANT EARS

by **Deena Sullivan**

illustrated by **Maruf Hanson**

Well, hello there my fine friends!
Welcome to this story.

It's not about dragons or handsome princes
fighting with glory.

It's about a little boy wise beyond his seven years.

Meet Finn J. Beloomey and his great big giant ears.

Let's take a look at Finn.
What do you see?

He's got nice brown eyes, shaggy brown hair, a
big wide smile, and...

YOWZA! Great big giant ears!

His mom and dad love him very much.

They take him to the beach and the park, but most importantly, they teach him lots of good stuff.

Like "Look both ways before you cross the street," "Be kind to others," and "Eat your veggies."

One day, his parents sat him down and said, "Finn, sometimes people can be not so nice. Maybe they didn't have a proper breakfast, maybe they didn't sleep so well, or maybe they are just having a blue day. But when they are mean, this is what you say..." Then they told him the magic words.

Magic?

Like hocus pocus, abracadabra, or open sesame? No, these magic words are much better and come with great mystical power. If you want to learn them, keep reading...

Finn has a sister named Fiona.
They have so much fun together.

They play tag with their friends in the park, make
blanket forts, and take turns bouncing Finn's super-
swirly colored ball he got for his birthday.

One summer day, Fiona was jumping rope with her best friends
in the whole world, Pam and Jenny. Finn walked by, bouncing
his swirly ball high in the air and whistling a catchy little song.

"Fiona," said Jenny. "Your brother's kind of cute. He's nice and
smart and carries the groceries for old Ms. Mary down the street.
But he has great big giant ears!"

"Yeah," added Pam.
"Those are some great big giant ears!"

"I know," said Fiona. Then she whispered the magic words her parents taught her.

"Oh!" said Jenny. "I guess I never thought about it that way. Do you think he'd come and play with us tomorrow?"

Should I tell you the magic words?
Are you ready yet?
Maybe not!

Let's keep reading about
Finn J. Beloomey and his
great big giant ears!

The Beloomeys lived next door to a family with twins the same age as Finn. Their names were Timmy and Tammy.

The twins loved to skip rocks and ride their shiny red bikes. But sadly, their favorite activity was making fun of kids at school, especially Finn Beloomey. Some people call them bullies, but the real name is "big meany weenies."

One day at school during lunchtime, Finn was playing soccer. He kicked the ball far and high and was running toward the goal when he heard Tammy yell out, "Hey Finn, you're so fast! It's probably because you have great big giant ears. I hope you don't fly away!"

Everyone in the schoolyard started laughing and pointing.

Finn felt sad for a moment and almost quit right then and there. But then he remembered his parents' words, and he held his head high and kept pumping his arms and legs as fast as he could, determined to score a goal.

As he came closer, he saw that Timmy (Tammy's big meany weenie brother) was the goalie. Timmy yelled out, "Yeah Finn, those really are some great big giant ears!"

Finn looked right at him, and with a little shrug and a grin, he said the magic words. His words surprised Timmy so much he didn't notice Finn had kicked the ball as hard as he could and it was flying over his head! Finn scored, and his team won the game!

Do you think you're ready now to hear the magic words?

Hmm, maybe not.
Keep reading!

Later that day after his favorite dinner of spaghetti and meatballs, Finn went outside to play with Fiona and Danny Mac, his best friend in the whole world.

They passed the house where Timmy and Tammy lived. Tammy was crying on the step. "What's wrong?" asked Finn.

"Who cares?" said Fiona. "Don't you remember how Tammy was a big meany weenie today?"

"I remember," said Finn. "But I also remember what my mom and dad say. 'You can't control how other people behave, you can only control how you behave.' And I want to behave nice!"

"Go away," said Tammy. "I don't want to talk about it."

But Finn sat down next to Tammy. "Maybe you'll feel better if you talk about it."

"Well," sniffed Tammy, "I was getting ready for gym class when these older girls came over and started making fun of me."

"What did they say?" asked Finn.

"It's so embarrassing. They...they..." sniffed Tammy. "They called me Big Toe Tammy!" She took off her sneaker and **yowza!** There it was—a really, really big toe.

"Tammy," said Finn, "remember when you and your brother made fun of me today?"

"Yes," said Tammy with a guilty look.

"And remember that I said something to your brother that surprised him so much he forgot to block the goal?"

"Yes," said Tammy. "I did wonder what you said."

Finn leaned closer and said, "What I'm about to tell you is the secret to handling **big meany weenies** like, um, yourself. If you learn these words and use them wisely, the **big meany weenies** just magically disappear."

Finn leaned over and whispered the magic words.

Are YOU ready to hear them?

Are you sure?

Well, come closer.

The magic words are...

Say it with me!

SO WHAT?!

Let's practice. "Hey, you have big feet!"

"SO WHAT?!"

"You have frizzy hair!"

"SO WHAT?!"

Tammy was amazed.
"Wow, two simple
words can change your
whole day."

"Yup," said Finn. "SO WHAT means I don't really care what you think. I know I have big ears, SO WHAT?! Everyone is different. Wouldn't it be silly and boring if we all looked the same? We'd have to wear name tags to tell each other apart. When I was little, this is what my parents taught me..."

My ears may be too big,

or they may be too small.

Who says what's right? Who says what's wrong?

My parents made me with help from above.

I'm nice and smart and have a life filled with love.

So you can laugh and point or whisper my name,

doesn't matter to me if it's all the same.

This is for you, my friends who at times don't fit in.

Take those silly comments with a shrug and a grin.

I know it can be hard to stand tall and proud

when you're a little different from the rest of the crowd.

But being unique makes you special and great,

it might be tough now, but just hang in and wait.

But if you're ever stuck or get in a rut,

repeat after me, loud and clear...

Yeah, I'm different,
SO WHAT?!